LET'S FIND OUT! PHYSICAL SCIENCE

WHAT IS ENERGY?

PAULA JOHANSON

Britannica® Educational Publishing

IN ASSOCIATION WITH

ROSEN EDUCATIONAL SERVICES

For Morgan, my energetic busy bee!

Published in 2015 by Britannica Educational Publishing (a trademark of Encyclopædia Britannica, Inc.) in association with The Rosen Publishing Group, Inc.
29 East 21st Street, New York, NY 10010

Distributed exclusively by Rosen Publishing.
To see additional Britannica Educational Publishing titles, go to rosenpublishing.com.

First Edition

Britannica Educational Publishing
J.E. Luebering: Director, Core Reference Group
Mary Rose McCudden: Editor, Britannica Student Encyclopedia

Rosen Publishing
Hope Lourie Killcoyne: Executive Editor
Isobel Towne: Editor
Nelson Sá: Art Director
Michael Moy: Designer
Cindy Reiman: Photography Manager
Amy Feinberg: Photo Research

Cataloging-in-Publication Data

Johanson, Paula, author.
What is energy?/Paula Johanson.—First edition.
pages cm.—(Let's find out! Physical science)
Includes bibliographical references and index.
ISBN 978-1-62275-492-2 (library bound)—ISBN 978-1-62275-494-6 (pbk.)—ISBN 978-1-62275-495-3 (6-pack)
1. Power (Mechanics)—Juvenile literature. 2. Force and energy—Juvenile literature. 3. Power resources—Juvenile literature. I. Title.
TJ163.95.J64 2015
531.6—dc23

2013048347

Manufactured in the United States of America

Photo Credits
Cover, p. 1 (flame) VikaSuh/Shutterstock.com; cover, p. 1, interior pages (fire border) Mikhail Bakunovich/Shutterstock.com; pp. 4, 5, 11, 12 Encyclopaedia Britannica, Inc.; p. 6 Ingram Publishing/Thinkstock; p. 7 Digital Vision/Photodisc/Thinkstock; p. 8 Harold Olejarz/iStock/Thinkstock; p. 9 jgorzynik/iStock/Thinkstock; pp. 13, 29 © AP Images; p. 14 stocksnapper/iStock/Thinkstock; p. 15 Purestock/Thinkstock; p. 16 Gilles Paire/iStock/Thinkstock; p. 17 Mikhail Malyshev/Hemera/Thinkstock; p. 18 Ralph Wetmore/Stone/Getty Images; p. 19 Clive Streeter/Dorling Kindersley/Getty Images; p. 20 United States Department of Energy; p. 21 Jeff Fusco/Getty Images; p. 22 NASA Courtesy of NASA/SDO and the AIA, EVE, and HMI science teams; p. 23 GoodMood Photo/iStock/Thinkstock; p. 24 ER Degginger/Science Source; p. 25 Stockbyte/Thinkstock; p. 26 Bloomberg/Getty Images; p. 27 Bent G. Nordeng/iStock/Thinkstock; p. 28 Paul Giamou/Stone/Getty Images.

Contents

DEFINING ENERGY

Energy is another word for power. Energy makes things move. It makes things warm. It also makes machines work and makes living things grow.

People use energy from many different sources. They use the power of wind, water, and sunlight. Plants and animals provide people with energy in the form of food. People also burn oil, coal, and natural gas for energy. They

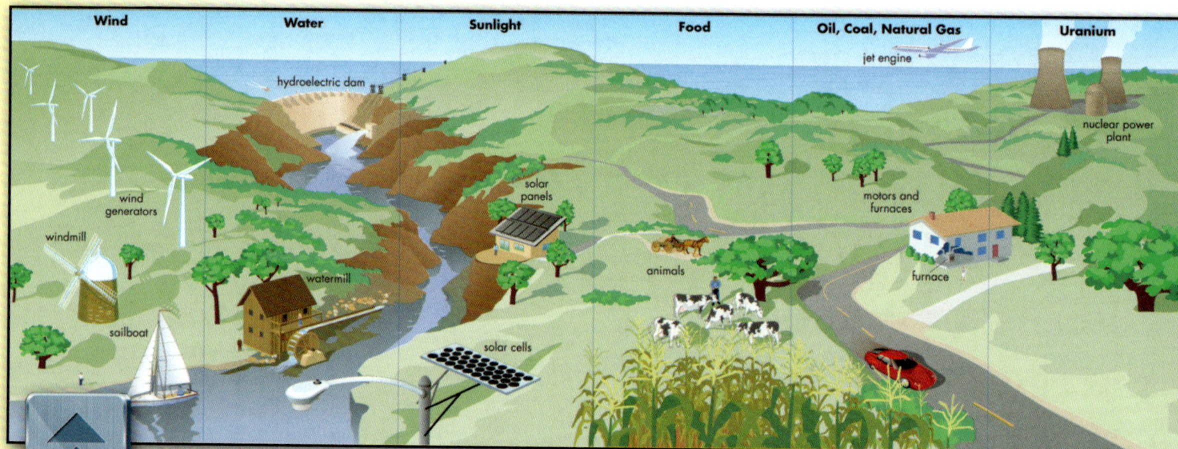

All over the world, energy is available in many forms. How many kinds of energy can you see suggested by this picture?

get nuclear energy from uranium.

Each of these forms of energy can be described as either potential energy or kinetic energy. Energy cannot be created or destroyed. It can only be changed from one form to another.

Energy is measured by how much work it does. People measure heat energy in units called joules or calories. The potential energy in electricity is measured in volts.

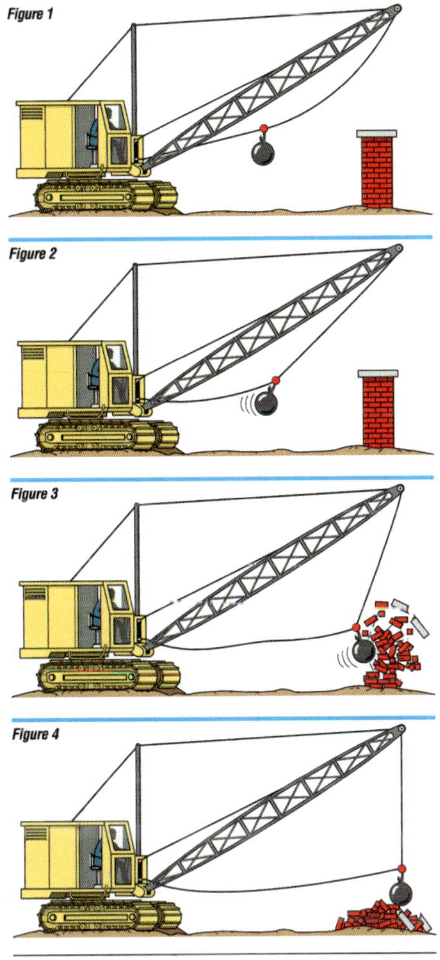

A wrecking crane uses energy to swing a heavy ball, and that ball delivers a powerful blow right on target!

KINETIC ENERGY

Kinetic energy is the energy of motion. The word "kinetic" means "active" and relates to the motion of physical objects. All moving objects have kinetic energy, even atoms. Atoms are the tiny building blocks that make up everything.

Forms of kinetic energy perform work.

The small movements of a jackhammer are kinetic energy. They have enough power to break concrete and rocks.

The work done by kinetic energy can be seen everywhere. River water has kinetic energy that can dig deep canyons as a river rushes downhill, pulled by gravity. Sailboats use the kinetic energy of wind to move them along. An electric fan uses the kinetic energy of its turning vanes to push air and make a breeze. Kinetic energy can turn turbines to power many kinds of machines.

A **turbine** is an engine that turns when its vanes are pushed by a moving fluid, such as air or water.

The blades of a wind turbine turn in the wind to make electricity for people to use.

Potential Energy

Potential energy is stored energy. An object with potential energy has the ability, or potential, to move. Potential energy comes from the position or the shape of an object.

Compare and Contrast

Potential energy comes in all kinds of forms. Compare and contrast kinds of potential energy. How are these forms of potential energy useful?

This boulder has the potential to tip over and roll downhill. It could smash things, but that energy is only potential while the boulder sits still.

Sometimes people store energy on purpose. Charging a battery, stretching a rubber band, and pushing down on a metal spring are all ways of storing energy. Sometimes energy builds up gradually. For example, a tree grows for many years before people cut it apart to burn for firewood. Potential energy is latent, or ready to be released, such as a rock perched high atop a cliff's edge. Only when it falls is its potential energy converted into kinetic energy.

Still or standing water has potential energy. The kinetic energy of water can be observed when a river runs downhill or over a drop.

Mechanical Energy

Mechanical energy is potential energy combined with kinetic energy. It is all the energy an object has because of its motion and position.

Machines use mechanical energy to do work. A hammer uses mechanical energy to drive nails into a board. When the hammer is raised, it has potential energy from the work done in lifting it. When the hammer is moved toward a nail, potential energy becomes kinetic energy, which does the work of driving the nail into a board. When the hammer hits the nail, energy is transferred to the nail and then to the board.

Think About It

A person stores potential energy by using a bow and arrow. The potential energy of stretching the bow is transferred to the arrow as kinetic energy when the bow is released.

Potential energy is stored energy, whereas kinetic energy is the energy of moving things. Tools are ways to harness potential and kinetic energy to generate mechanical energy.

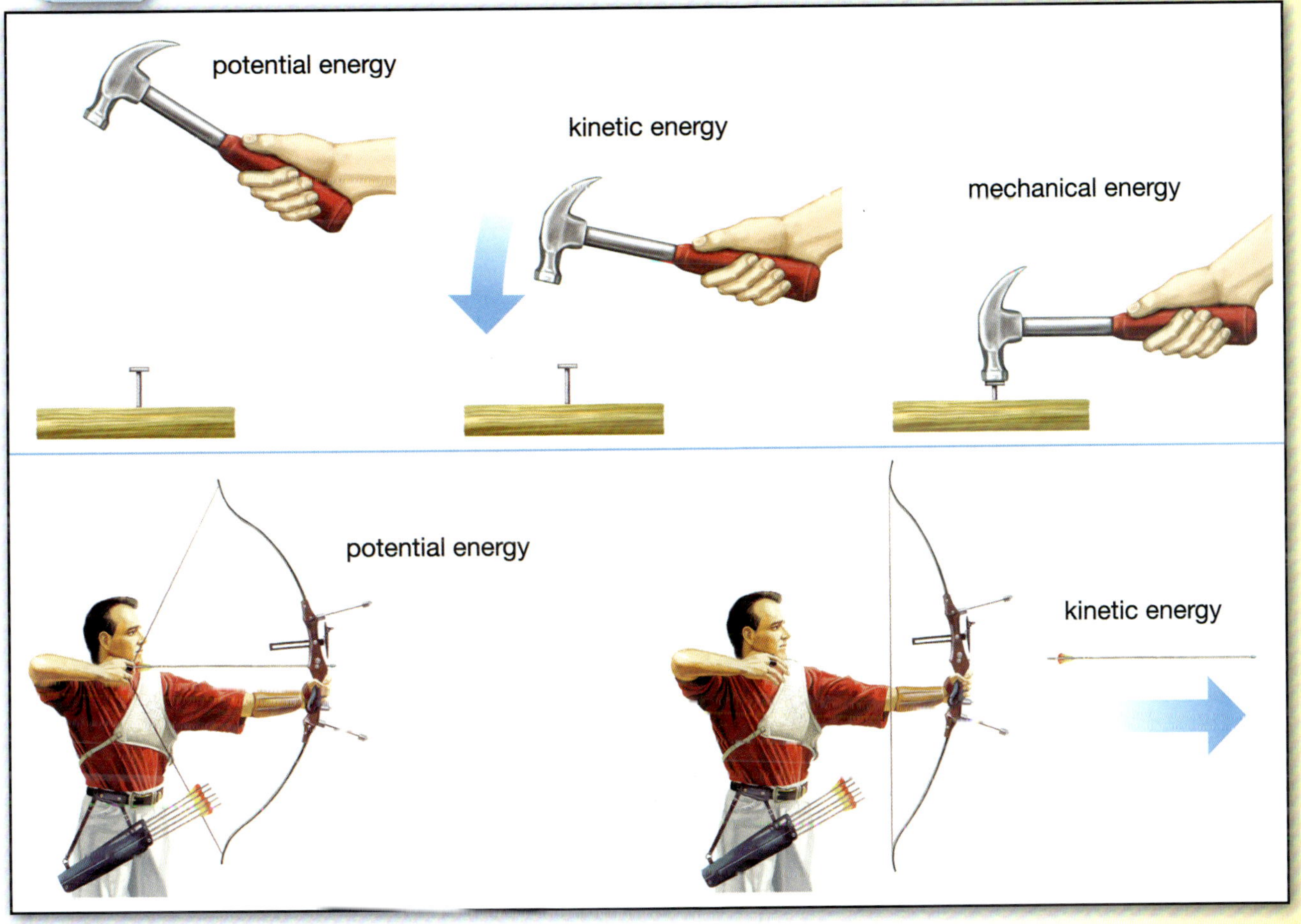

Changing Forms of Energy

One form of energy can be changed into another. Energy cannot be created, but it cannot be destroyed either. Sometimes people change energy into a form that is easier to use.

A tree changes energy from sunlight into chemical energy. An automobile changes chemical energy into mechanical and heat energy. A nuclear reaction changes nuclear

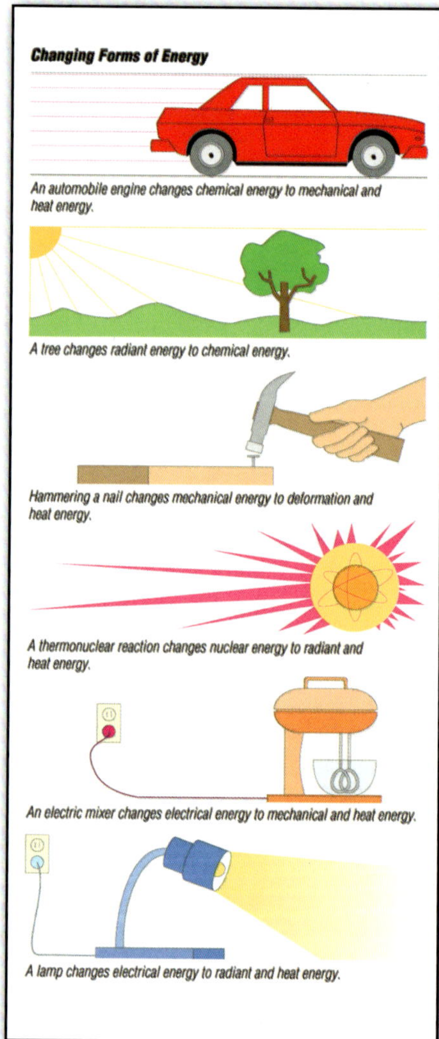

Some forms of energy are easy to change. Sometimes people need special tools or careful work to use certain kinds of energy.

energy to radiant and heat energy. An electric mixer changes electrical energy to mechanical and heat energy. A lamp changes electrical energy to radiant and heat energy. People invent all kinds of ways to use energy in its various forms.

COMPARE AND CONTRAST

Compare automobiles with carts pulled by horses. What kinds of stored energy are being changed to do the work? Why would people choose to use a cart or an automobile?

Automobiles use fossil fuels but contribute to pollution, while horses eat plants and make reusable waste.

Heat Energy

Heat energy causes the atoms of a substance to move or vibrate faster. This increases the temperature of the substance. Heat energy can be used on purpose, such as to make stoves hot for cooking or to let matches start a crackling fire. It can be dangerous if heat energy starts a fire where people don't expect it.

For many years, some people have used hot water and steam from inside Earth

The chemical reaction of striking a match to start a fire releases a lot of heat energy.

to warm their houses. They run the hot water or steam in pipes underneath their floors to provide heat. This kind of heat energy is known as geothermal energy.

Think About It

Winter clothes don't give a person heat energy. The person's body gives heat energy to the clothes! Then the clothes keep that heat from blowing away by trapping it against the body.

When people feel cold, sometimes the answer is to wear layered clothes that hold in body heat.

Chemical Energy

When some atoms are mixed, they bind together in new ways. This is a chemical reaction. Chemical reactions can use energy or they can release it. Often

Think About It

Chemicals inside a battery store energy. When batteries are used, chemical energy changes into electric energy. Why would people need to make batteries?

Chemical energy stored inside batteries can be turned into electric energy.

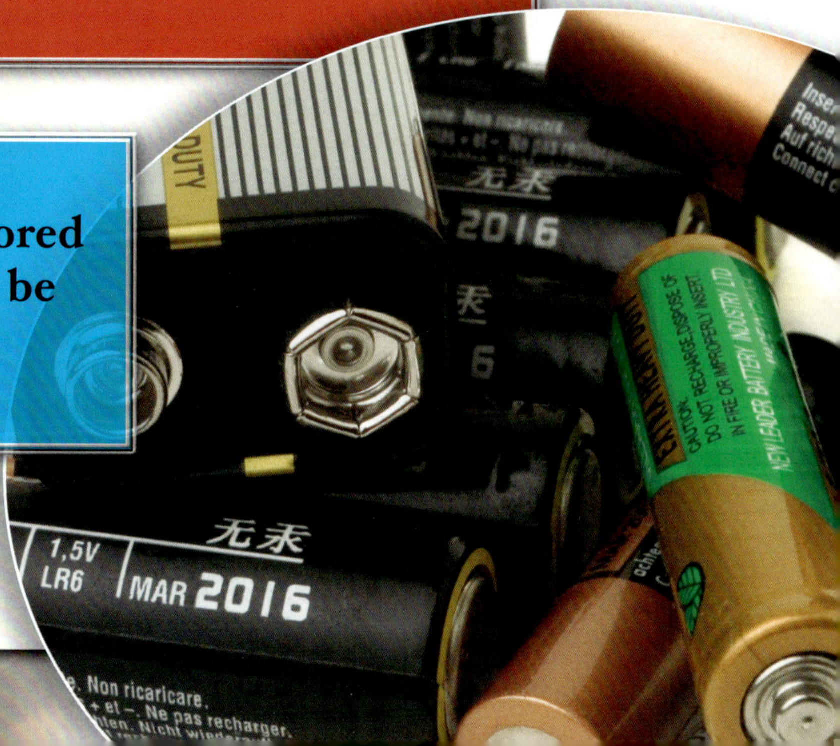

the energy is in the form of heat.

Plants use energy from sunlight to bind together atoms from air and water so that they can grow. Sunlight energy is used in the chemical rcaction, but it doesn't just disappear. It changes into stored chemical energy in the body of plants. When animals eat plants, they turn the chemical energy into energy that they use to live and move. When fire burns wood or oil, that's another chemical reaction. Lots of heat energy is released quickly!

When animals and people eat, they change chemical energy from food into mechanical energy and heat energy.

ELECTRICAL ENERGY

Electricity is the flow of tiny particles called electrons from one atom to another. In nature, electricity can be seen in bolts of lightning. Lightning is a large number of electrons flowing through air all at once. Lightning releases huge amounts of energy.

Scientists have learned how to generate, or make, electricity from other forms of energy. Electricity is

Bolts of lightning move huge amounts of energy from one raincloud to another or from a cloud to the ground.

useful because it can be sent through wires to where it is needed. It powers heaters, lightbulbs, and computers. Electricity doesn't make smoke or ashes as chemical energy does when wood, coal, or oil are burned. Today, electricity provides most of the energy to run machines.

The word "**electricity**" comes from the Greek word for a fossil called amber. When amber is rubbed, it gains an electric charge. Then it can attract and hold little bits of fluff.

Electric charges are not all as big as lightning bolts. Little charges build up and can be released, too, as when amber is rubbed.

Nuclear Energy

The energy that holds together the nucleus of an atom is called nuclear, or atomic, energy. Atoms are the basic building blocks of matter. When nuclear energy is released, it changes into other forms, including heat and light. Nuclear energy can be released through fission, when the nucleus of an atom splits into two or more

Think About It

Nuclear power plants are useful. But nuclear waste remains dangerous for thousands of years. Is any kind of energy too dangerous or harmful to use?

This explosion of an atomic bomb in 1952 is a vivid demonstration of nuclear energy—the energy contained in the atomic nucleus.

Power plants are built in areas where people need them most. Cities use a lot of electricity and require a lot of energy to power their buildings and systems.

parts, or through fusion, when two nuclei join to form a single nucleus.

Nuclear energy was first used in very powerful bombs that the United States used during the Second World War. Nuclear power plants heat water to make steam and turn turbines, creating electricity. Some nuclear power plants also make radioactive pellets for use in medical machines and treatments.

SOLAR ENERGY

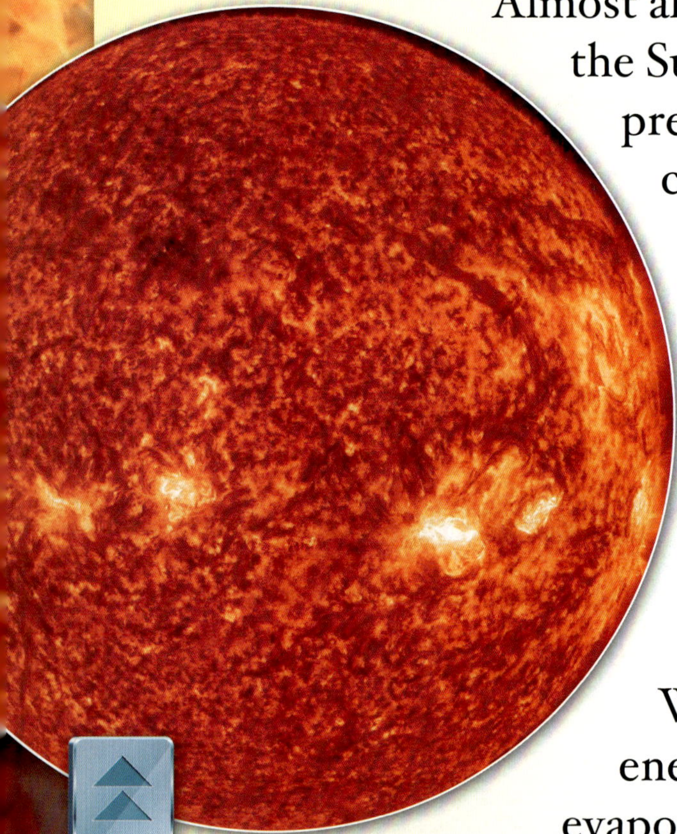

Heat from nuclear reactions inside the Sun stirs hot gases, like a boiling pot of soup on a stove.

Almost all energy on Earth comes from the Sun. At the Sun's core, great pressure squeezes hydrogen gas, causing a nuclear reaction. Atoms of hydrogen join together to make helium—and lots of energy! That energy radiates into space as sunlight.

On Earth, the Sun's light warms the air and causes the wind to move. Wind helps carry that heat energy around the world. Water evaporates when solar energy heats lakes and oceans.

People use solar energy in many different

Sunshine and wind dry wet laundry on a clothesline. That's a passive solar-power system.

Compare and Contrast

What other kinds of solar energy projects can you name? Why would people use solar power instead of burning fuel?

ways. Solar panels change radiant energy into electricity. Passive solar energy projects use sunlight more directly. Hanging laundry on a line to dry in the sunshine is an example of using passive solar energy.

Fossil-Fuel Energy

People have always used plants and animal fats as fuel for fires. But there are other fuels as well. When plants and ocean plankton die, they decay, or break down. Long ago some remains became deeply buried and underwent a slow chemical reaction over millions of years to create what are

The remains of an enormous number of tiny creatures like this krill were buried long ago and slowly formed fossil fuels.

The word "**fossil**" means "dug up." Fossils are the remains of living things from very long ago, buried as sedimentary rock formed. Taken from the ground, fossil fuels run automobiles and airplanes.

called fossil fuels. Petroleum, natural gas, and coal are all examples of fossil fuels.

Fossil fuels store chemical energy. These fuels burn in a fast chemical reaction that releases heat energy very quickly. The reaction also makes smoke, soot, and harmful gases. The heat energy is used to run factories, heat homes, and power engines.

When fossil fuels release chemical energy, they also create smoke, soot, and harmful gases, which can be dangerous.

Alternative Energy

Fossil fuels pollute air when they are used. They are also being used up much too quickly. Scientists are in search of other sources of energy to replace fossil fuels.

Some alternative energy sources have been used for many years. These include sunlight, wind, rivers and oceans,

Fuel can be made from green algae and other ordinary things!

and heat from inside Earth. Some biofuels are made from plants, such as soybeans, or from organisms called algae.

Most alternative energy sources are renewable. Unlike fossil fuels, most alternative energy sources are not likely to run out. These energy sources can be used to generate electricity, heat water, and fuel vehicles.

Hydropower is the energy from moving water. Flowing water can be used to turn turbines to generate electricity. Turbines can also be turned by ocean waves or ocean tides.

Niagara Falls is a major source of hydropower.

Energy Everywhere

Energy is everywhere, in many different forms. The Sun radiates energy out into space. Energy from the Sun's light mixes Earth's air and water. Solar energy changes form as wind and water move around the world. Even Earth's core is warm, from gravity pressure and uranium radiation. There is plenty of potential energy and kinetic energy changing form all the time.

With a simple frame, greenhouses trap energy from the Sun to grow plants.

All that energy makes Earth a good place for all kinds of living things. People can use energy in ways that are renewable. However, people can also use energy in ways that create pollution and waste. Creating and using energy wisely is one of humanity's greatest challenges.

Think About It

Many people feel we need to develop cleaner and more renewable energy sources for the health of our planet. Should we try alternative energy sources or just use less fossil fuels? Or both?

Harnessing one's own potential, kinetic, and mechanical energy for the good of the planet is energy well spent!

GLOSSARY

atoms The smallest particles of an element that can exist either alone or in combination.

batteries Chemical-energy storage devices.

calories Units for measuring heat energy, especially for the energy released from food.

chemical reaction A process in which a substance changes into a different substance.

coal A fossil fuel formed from plants of long ago that were trapped under deep layers of rock.

electrons Negatively charged elementary particles that travel around the nucleus of an atom or through wires in electric circuits.

fossil fuels Fuels made from ancient plant and animal life that is pressed under layers of rock for millions of years.

geothermal Relating to heat energy from deep inside Earth.

hydrogen A colorless, odorless gas; the lightest element.

joules Units for measuring energy, especially for heat energy.

light Radiant electromagnetic energy that can be seen.

nuclear reaction A change in the identity or characteristics of an atomic nucleus, produced by bombarding it with an energetic particle.

plankton Tiny living organisms that float in the ocean in large numbers.

power The rate at which energy is transferred.

radiant energy Energy that radiates from a source in waves.

radioactive Giving off energy by the breaking apart of atoms of certain elements.

sedimentary Formed from sediment that settles at the bottom of a lake or ocean.

solar energy Radiant energy from the Sun.

uranium A heavy metal that is a radioactive element.

volts Units for measuring the potential energy in electricity.

For More Information

Books

Aloian, Molly. *Green Energy.* New York, NY: Crabtree Publishing, 2013.

Challoner, Jack. *Energy: Eyewitness Books*. London, England: DK Publishing, 2012.

Guillain, Charlotte. *Saving Energy.* Portsmouth, NH: Heinemann Publishing/Acorn, 2008.

Mulder, Michelle. *Brilliant! Shining a Light on Sustainable Energy.* Victoria, BC, Canada: Orca Book Publishers, 2013.

Spilbury, Louise. *Energy*. Portsmouth, NH: Heinemann Publishing, 2013.

Zuchora-Walske, Christine. *The Transfer of Energy.* North Mankato, MN: Cherry Lake Publishing, 2013.

Websites

Because of the changing nature of Internet links, Rosen Publishing has developed an online list of websites related to the subject of this book. This site is updated regularly. Please use this link to access the list:

http://www.rosenlinks.com/lfo/energy

INDEX